Rabbit's Rainy Day

By Amye Rosenberg

A Golden Book • New York
Western Publishing Company, Inc., Racine, Wisconsin 53404

Father looked out the window.
"It is raining cats and dogs,"
he said.
Pinky looked, too.
All he saw was rain.

"Where are the cats and dogs?"
asked Pinky.
"They are in their houses,"
said Mother.
"That is just a saying.
Today you must stay indoors, too."

Pinky did not like
to stay indoors.
"There is nothing to do,"
said Pinky.
"Then find something to do,"
said Father.

Sister was reading a book.
Brother was building a toy boat.

So Pinky made something, too.

He cut.
He colored.
He folded paper.

"Look at my airplane!"
said Pinky.

"Watch it fly!"
he said.

Then Pinky found a bag.
So he made something else.

"Boo!"
said Pinky.

Then Pinky saw a ball.
It belonged to Brother.
Brother let Pinky play with it.

Pinky threw the ball.

Brother was wet.
He was also mad.

He ran after Pinky.
They ran down the stairs.

They ran into Mother.

"Wash up,"
said Mother.
"We will eat lunch soon."

Pinky washed.

Then he went to the kitchen.

Father was making lunch.

He filled a bowl with vegetables.

Pinky opened a jar.
Inside was peanut butter.
"I will help you with lunch,"
said Pinky.

Father cut the bread.

Pinky helped with lunch.

After lunch Father took a nap.
Mother rested in a chair.

Sister closed her eyes.
Brother took a nap, too.
The house was quiet.

Pinky sat on his bed.
He did not want to sleep.
He wanted to have fun.

He saw Brother's band hat.
He saw Brother's drum.

Pinky put on the band hat.
He picked up the drum.

Pinky played marching band.
He marched all over.
He banged the drum.

"Boom! Boom!"
went the drum.
Father jumped up.
The noise woke Mother.

"Boom! Boom!"
went the drum.
Sister fell to the floor.
Brother woke up, too.

Then Pinky ran to the window.
The rain had stopped.
The sun was shining.
"Now I can play outside!"
said Pinky.

Mother and Father were happy.
Brother and Sister were happy.

But most of all
Pinky was happy.